AN ALMOST VERY SCARY DAY

by Judy Ann Lowe

Illustrated by Ayuna Collins & David Edward Martin

J.S. Pathways, Dallas, Texas

Illustrations by Ayuna Collins and David Edward Martin

Layout and design by Carolyn Oakley, Luminous Moon Design

Published by J.S. Pathways

Printed in the United States

ISBN-13: 978-1519163998
ISBN-10: 1519163998

Dedication

To my Little White Light and my lovable Sam,

who have brought me hope, joy, and purpose.

– Judy

We dedicate the illustrations in this book to our late

feline sister Shorty Rojas. All dogs may go to heaven,

but that's only if the cats let them in.

– Ayuna & David

Inspiration

The inspiration for this story is the real-life event

that happened with Judy's parakeet, named Mr. Blue,

when she was a little girl and the continued presence

of the Little White Light in Judy's adult life.

Every night, before falling asleep, Penny would say good night to her secret friend, the Little White Light. Since it first starting appearing to her, it always showed up in the corner of the ceiling, both at night and in the early morning hours, and would blink, reassuring her that it was there.

One night, after turning off the bedside lamp, Penny called to her special Little White Light, but there was no answer. It wasn't there.

She waited. When it didn't show itself, she called out to it saying, "Hello?

"Hello, my Little Light?

"Hello, hello, hello."

When the Little Light still didn't appear, Penny wondered where it had gone. "Where are you my Little Light?" she said sleepily.

As she began to fall asleep, Penny noticed something high up in the corner of the room. The Little White Light blinked, and Penny knew it could tell what she was thinking and feeling.

"There you are," she said. "I see you. You are a part of me, Little Light. I'm so glad you came into my life." Then, she could finally go to sleep.

The next day was sunny and beautiful so Penny decided to work in her backyard garden. As she worked with the spinach, baby salad greens, kale, flowers, and tomatoes, she thought about the Little Light being late several times. Perhaps it was sleeping, like she was, or maybe visiting with other little lights.

"After all," Penny thought, "everyone and everything needs to be with family and friends, every now and then."

Penny continued to think about the Little Light's absence. She hoped that it would come back to her when it heard her asking or calling for it.

While Penny was working in the garden, MJ, her best friend who lived next door, came over to see Penny. He could tell that something was on her mind.

"What are you thinking about?" MJ asked.

Penny had never told anyone about the Little White Light before, but she was so worried about the Little Light being gone, she just had to tell someone. MJ was her best friend and she knew she could trust him with her secret.

As Penny told MJ about the Little White Light and how it appeared to her every night and every morning, he listened enthusiastically, getting more and more excited. Then, he smiled in wonder and awe.

"Really? That's so great," he said excitedly. His mind whirled with a million questions. "Do other people see it? Does it follow you to school? Does anyone else know?"

Penny laughed, glad that MJ was as excited about the Little White Light as she was. "No one else I know has seen it," she told him. "And no, it doesn't follow me to school. At least not yet! You're the first person I've told, because you're my best friend."

MJ beamed.

Suddenly, MJ and Penny heard a terrible noise—a frightening screeching and squawking.

MJ ran around to the side of the house where the horrible sound was coming from. He called out, "Penny come quick!"

Penny ran to him and, after she rounded the corner of the house, saw a sight that made her gasp. It was a cat with a mouthful of feathers!

"Oh no!" she cried out. The cat had caught a bird.

"You poor little thing," Penny said. She felt so sorry for the little bird.

MJ saw the cat had a collar and so he knew it was safe to get close to it. He got down on the ground right in front of the cat and started talking to it.

"Let the bird go," he said, trying to keep his voice calm.

"Can't you see you're hurting it?

"You really don't want to eat that bird.

"You're a good cat.

"Relax your jaw and let the bird go."

Penny watched the cat and the bird while listening to MJ's reassuring voice.

Again MJ said to the cat, "Let the bird go. Relax your jaw and let the bird go!"

Slowly, MJ reached out his hand and began to tickle the cat's belly. The cat jerked its head, blinked its eyes several times, opened its mouth and meowed. As soon as the cat opened its mouth, the bird fluttered out.

Penny was so impressed with MJ. He always saw the good in everything and tried to do the right thing, even when he was afraid.

When Penny saw the bird, she realized it was a beautiful, blue parakeet. The poor little thing was so afraid, it didn't even try to fly away.

Very slowly, MJ reached over. The parakeet let MJ pick it up. He held it in his lap, giving it comfort. MJ was so happy. He had just rescued another living thing from a very frightening situation.

Penny was so proud of MJ, and yet she was worried about the bird. Would it survive?

The cat stayed there for a few moments watching MJ, Penny and the bird. Then it stood up and started to walk away. It stopped, turned around, and gave one more look over its shoulder. Finally, it went on its way with its swishing tail disappearing into the tall grass.

Penny and MJ took the parakeet into Penny's house. She breathlessly told her Dad everything that had happened with the cat, the bird and how MJ had saved the day. "Do you think the bird will be ok, Dad?"

"I don't know, Penny," her Dad said. "How about you and MJ get the old bird cage from the garage and make a nice, safe place for him to rest."

Penny and MJ ran to get the cage. They cleaned it up and gently put the parakeet inside. MJ, Penny and her Dad watched the parakeet. Its sides were heaving up and down as it struggled to breathe.

"I hope he's going to be okay," Penny said.

"Me too," said MJ.

They all watched the parakeet together for a long time. His feathers were such a beautiful blue color.

"Maybe we should give him a name," MJ said.

Penny nodded. She looked at his blue feathers. It looked like he was wearing a little blue suit.

"I've got it," she said. "Let's call him *Mr. Blue.*"

"That's perfect," MJ said.

He looked at the clock and was surprised to see how late it was.

"Well, I have to go home for dinner now," he said, rubbing his rumbling tummy. "I'll come back tomorrow to see how Mr. Blue is feeling. Bye, Penny. 'Night, Mr. Blue."

Later that night, when it was time to go to bed, Dad placed a cover over the cage.

"This will help Mr. Blue go to sleep," he said.

"Good night, Mr. Blue," Penny whispered. Then she turned off the living room lights, went to her bedroom and climbed into bed.

Penny looked up to where the Little White Light usually appeared. Hoping to see her friend, she started calling to it.

"Hello, Little Light?

"Hello, my Little Light.

"Hello, hello, hello?"

Still the Little Light didn't appear. Penny rolled over and hugged her teddy bear. She felt a little lonely.

"What a big day," she thought. "That was so scary and MJ was so brave."

Still wondering where the Little White Light was, she began to drift off to sleep.

"I hope Mr. Blue will be all better tomorrow," she thought sleepily and made a wish on the first star she saw out her window.

The next morning, Penny woke up and looked to the corner of her ceiling. She still didn't see the Little White Light!

"Maybe it's visiting friends," Penny thought, changing into her clothes.

As she ran to check on Mr. Blue, the doorbell rang.

"How is Mr. Blue?" MJ asked, bursting through the door. "Is his wing ok?"

"I don't know," Penny answered, "I was just going to check on him. Let's look together!"

Penny and MJ ran into the living room.

Penny took the cover off the cage and Mr. Blue chirped as if to say, "Good morning."

Overjoyed, Penny opened the cage and out hopped Mr. Blue.

Mr. Blue shook his wings, looked around, and flew all over the room.

Penny and MJ laughed and clapped their hands at Mr. Blue's antics. They were so happy he was feeling better!

All of a sudden, Mr. Blue flew up into the corner of the ceiling where Penny saw the blink of a light.

"Why, hello Little Light!" she called joyfully. The Little White Light had returned.

MJ saw Penny looking at the ceiling. He looked up and was so surprised.

"Is that the Little Light you were telling me about, Penny?"

"Yes," she said. "Can you see it too? No one else has ever seen it before." As they both looked at the glowing light, a feeling of happiness and contentment came over them. It was as though everything was right with the world.

"Wow," MJ said in awe. "It's so beautiful and mesmerizing."

As soon as he said that, two more lights appeared. One was large and foggy-looking while the other one was small and bright. Penny and MJ could not believe what they had just seen. Two more Little Lights!

"Now I know where you've been, Little Light," Penny said. "You've been making new friends. I'm so glad we can all be friends together."

Everything in Penny's life was getting better and better. Now Penny knew she didn't have to worry if the Little Light didn't answer when she called. It was off playing with its friends and would appear when she really needed it.

Penny and her friends—even the cat—played together all the time. Their days were filled with great adventures.

Blink!

Flicker!

Glow!

The End

About Parakeets & Budgies

The parakeet is a popular cage bird that, in captivity, is raised in many different colors and found in any pet store in green, blue, yellow, and white. In America, we call them parakeets. However, they are native to Australia and live in large flocks in Australia's dry outback. There, they are called budgerigars, or budgies, and are naturally green.

Parakeets have been raised in captivity since the 1850's. They are like small parrots with long feathery tails. Some people like to think of them as members of the cockatoo family. These small, wonderful pets have been charming people for many years not only because of their color, but because they are healthy, happy, friendly, have playful personalities and are sociable, curious, and intelligent.

The average parakeet is about seven inches long and weighs about as much as a slice of bread. Its wingspan is between 10 and 14 inches. For exercise, they love to stretch. They also like to preen themselves to stay clean. This helps to keep their feathers in good shape. After preening, parakeets will fluff themselves to get their feathers back in order. Sometimes, they do this right before they take a nap. Speaking of naps, parakeets will nap for 15 to 45 minutes every day. They will also yawn before or after their nap.

The male parakeet is the best talker, but both male and female can learn words, phrases, and to whistle well. Parakeets can live up to ten years. They make great companions, bond with their keeper, mimic the sounds of their surroundings, and quickly learn tricks. A parakeet can be a wonderful pet.

Acknowledgments

With great appreciation to Carolyn Oakley

for her expertise with book layout and creative direction;

Ayuna Collins and David Edward Martin for their artistic creativity;

Aleanna Collins for her editing skills;

and Karen Gresham Nickell for her unending

support, ideas, and motivation.

About the Author

Judy Lowe is a retired Gifted and Talented teacher in the Dallas Independent School District in Dallas, Texas. Since 1966, she has earned a Bachelor's Degree in Music Education, a Masters Degree in Elementary Education and a Certificate in Gifted and Talented Education. Her hobbies are reading, working in the yard, walking, and being outside.

Judy enjoys musicals, attending The Vocal Majority performances, traveling, and watching many programs on PBS, the Hallmark Channel and the History Channel. She currently serves on the Board of Directors of the North Texas Book Festival and is a member of the Dallas Museum of Art, Texas Retired Teachers Association, Dallas ISD TAG Educators Alumni, KERA and the Texas Association of Authors.

Judy's first book, *The Little White Light*, is a 2016 Book Excellence Award Winner and a *Readers Favorite* Five Star selection. Her second book, *MJ's New Friend,* received second place in the 2015 North Texas Book Festival for Children's Books Ages 6-12 and *An Almost Very Scary Day* is a 2016 Book Excellence Award Finalist and a *Readers Favorite* Five Star selection.

Visit Judy online at JSPathways.com and Facebook.com/JSPathways.

About the Artists

Ayuna Collins attended California Institute of the Arts where she was a double major in Dance and Animation. While at CalArts, Ayuna began studying with E. Michael Mitchell. She completed her studies at the San Francisco Art Institute (B.F.A. 2013). Ayuna lives and works in Boulder, Colorado, investigating the interplay between her performing and visual arts.

David Edward Martin is a North Carolina-born artist and educator. He is formally trained in filmmaking, graphic design, and fine art. His interminable curiosity leads him to pursue projects of a diverse nature, all the while seeking out the nuanced connections between various modes of expression, both as an artist and a human being.

He holds an MFA from Art Center College of Design, and lives and works in Los Angeles.

Enjoy these other award-winning books by Judy Ann Lowe!

Available at Amazon.com, BarnesandNoble.com, Indielector.store
and from the publisher at JSPathways.com

Learn more about Judy's books, see a schedule of her upcoming events, and
enjoy videos and photos at JSPathways.com and Facebook.com/JSPathways

Made in the USA
Monee, IL
24 September 2021